I0565942

Published in Great Britain by L.R. Price Publications Ltd., 2023.

27 Old Gloucester Street,

London,

WC1N 3AX

www.lrpricepublications.com

Cover artwork by L.R. Price Publications Ltd.

Used under exclusive and unlimited licence by L.R. Price Publications Ltd.

ISBN-13: 978-1-915330-33-8

Animals of Ferndale Forest

Maria Gregory

CHAPTER 1
JACKDAW'S VOICE

Jackdaw opened his eyes to a glorious day. He stood up in his nest, ruffled his feathers, stretched his neck, opened his beak and 'sang', "CAW, CAW, CAW." It was an awful sound. Sammy Squirrel who had been sound asleep in his cosy hole in the same tree, was woken with such a start at Jackdaw's 'song', that he had to put his paws over his ears, but this hardly helped at all. He could still hear Jackdaw's 'CAW, CAW, CAW'.

Sammy went to the front of his hole and looked up into the branches. "JACKDAW," he shouted, but Jackdaw was still 'singing' at the top of his voice. Sammy ran up the tree to Jackdaw's branch. The sound was really bad. He put his paws over his ears and shouted, "JACKDAW." Jackdaw turned around, saw Sammy and stopped 'singing'.

"Sammy!" Jackdaw exclaimed, "isn't it a lovely morning?" Sammy folded his arms and looked at Jackdaw.

"It was," Sammy said. Jackdaw was confused; Sammy seemed annoyed.

"What do you mean?" he said.

"You were making too much noise," said Sammy.

"Noise, what noise?" Jackdaw did not understand.

"You, your noise." Jackdaw could see that Sammy was very annoyed but still did not know why. He stared at Sammy for a bit, then it came to him.

"Oh!" he exclaimed, "you mean my singing. Was I too loud? I'm sorry." Sammy began to laugh.

"Singing," he said and laughed even harder, "you call that dreadful noise singing?"

"Dreadful?" Jackdaw was shocked, "you think my singing is dreadful?" He was feeling sad.

"Singing Jackdaw!" said Sammy, through gulps of laughter. "You could not call what you were doing singing, you sounded more like a dog with a sore throat. Ask anyone in the forest, you just can't sing." And with that, Sammy Squirrel ran down the tree to his hole leaving a very sad Jackdaw behind him.

Jackdaw settled down in his nest. He began to think about what Sammy had said. 'Was it true? Was Sammy right: he really couldn't sing?' Jackdaw ruffled his feathers. "I can sing," he said out loud, but he wasn't really convinced.

Sitting in his nest he came to a decision. 'I shall ask the other animals,' and off he went. He flew to Mr and Mrs Rabbit's house. He knocked on the door. Mrs Rabbit opened the door she was surprised to see Jackdaw standing there. "Why Jackdaw, what brings you here? We were just having breakfast; would you like to join us?"

"Yes, that would be nice, thank you," said Jackdaw and he went inside the cosy house. Sitting at the table was Mr Rabbit, Jenny Rabbit, Rufus Rabbit, Lisa Rabbit, Billy Rabbit and baby Rabbit. Mr Rabbit smiled at Jackdaw as he came in.

"'Ullo Jackdaw," he said, "joining us for breakfast?"

"If that's all right?" said Jackdaw.

"No problem," Mr Rabbit replied.

"Hello children," said Jackdaw.

"Hello Mr Jackdaw," chorused the children.

"Sit yourself down Jackdaw," said Mrs Rabbit, as she placed a plate of hot, buttered toast in front of him. After eating, he wiped his beak and cleared his voice. "Could I ask you something?" Mr and Mrs Rabbit looked each other then looked at Jackdaw.

"Certainly, what is it?"

"What do you think of my singing?" he asked.

"Your singing?" Mr Rabbit looked uncomfortable.

"Yes," said Jackdaw, "do you think I can sing? Does it sound nice?" Mr and Mrs Rabbit looked at each other. They had heard Jackdaw most mornings and knew how bad he sounded, but not wanting to upset him they said,

"Of course you can sing, you sound lovely." Jackdaw was pleased. Then suddenly, Lisa Rabbit said,

"Ooo Daddy, you said you wished Jackdaw would lose his voice, 'cos he sounds so bad." Mr Rabbit looked embarrassed.

"Shush Lisa," said Mrs Rabbit and she led her to the bedroom. Jackdaw was devastated. Mr Rabbit put an arm around Jackdaw's shoulders.

"Lisa got a bit mixed up. What I said was it would be a pity if you were to lose your voice, isn't that right Mrs Rabbit?"

"Yes, yes that's right Jackdaw. You know how children are, they often hear things wrong," and they gently steered him towards the door. Jackdaw nodded his head.

"Yes, I suppose they do," but deep down he knew Lisa Rabbit was telling the truth. He said goodbye and flew into the air.

Flying above the trees he began to reason with himself. 'How would forest animals know if he could sing? Only other birds will be able to tell him if he can sing.' He felt more cheerful. 'That's what I must do, I must ask the birds.' He felt much better now and off he went to find some other birds. During his flight he met many birds but they were too busy to talk to him. Jackdaw was about to give up when he spotted a group of birds feeding on the ground. He flew down and landed just outside the group. There was a mixture of sparrows, pigeons and starlings. Jackdaw approached them slowly. "Excuse me," he said. The birds stopped feeding and looked at him. One very fat wood pigeon walked towards him.

"Coo-ould we help you-oo?"

"Please, if you would." Two sparrows hopped over to him.

"Are you in trouble? How can we help?" they said together.

"Can you tell me if I can sing?" Jackdaw asked.

"Most certainly," the starlings chipped in. They had been listening to the conversation. "When would you like to try?" said the birds.

"Well, there's no time like the present," said Jackdaw. The birds stood in their group and waited. Jackdaw ruffled his feathers, took a deep breath, opened his beak And … "CAW, CAW, CAW."

The sparrows jumped at the noise and flapped their wings in fright, the starlings began to laugh, only the pigeons remained silent. Jackdaw carried on until the fat wood pigeon walked over to him and put a wing over his beak. "I'm so-oo very sorry but I had to-oo stop you-oo." Jackdaw looked at the fat wood pigeon sadly.

"Was it that bad?"

"'Fraid so old boy," said the pigeon, "but don't let it get youoo down. There are many birds that can't sing: Magpie and Crow are but a few-oo."

"I bet they're not as bad as me," said Jackdaw and tears began to roll down his face. Before the fat wood pigeon could say another word, Jackdaw took to the sky. The other birds watched as he flew away.

"I do hope he is all right," said one little sparrow and all the others nodded.

Jackdaw was on his way back to his nest. 'I will never ever try to sing again.' he decided. When he landed in his tree he went to his nest and put his head under his wing feeling very sad.

The next day, Sammy Squirrel woke up. He listened for Jackdaw but heard nothing; it was blissful. He looked out of his hole and stared up into the branches but there was no sign of Jackdaw. "Coo-ee Sammy, lovely morning isn't it?" Sammy looked down. It was Diana Deer.

"Morning Diana, yes it is lovely, especially since Jackdaw's being quiet." Diana Deer laughed.

"Yes, he did sound awful didn't he? Well must be off, see you," and off she ran into the woods. Sammy went to the base of the tree to collect some nuts. While he was there Mrs Rabbit hopped by.

"Hello, Sammy," she said, "isn't it lovely and peaceful?"

"Yes, isn't it?" he agreed.

"I'm just stocking up my larder."

"I know," said Mrs Rabbit, "it's never ending. I'm off to Farmer Giles, he's got some lovely vegetables growing in his garden."

"You be careful," said Sammy.

"I will be," she said and off she went.

Meanwhile, up in his nest, Jackdaw had heard every word. Feeling very hurt, he suddenly made up his mind to leave the wood and find somewhere else to live, but first he had to find another tree and build a nest. He flew high into the air and out of the wood. He began to look down towards the ground for a new home. He flew over Farmer Giles' farm and saw Mrs Rabbit in his garden picking vegetables. She had said it was peaceful now he had stopped singing. Jackdaw sniffed and flew on towards the valley and the town. He had been flying for about twenty minutes and had not found a tree he liked. He decided to return to the wood. "I'll try again tomorrow," he said. He was just flying back over Farmer Giles' garden when he looked down and what he saw made him stop in his tracks. There was Mrs Rabbit clutching her vegetables, trapped against the fence by a huge dog. His fur was up, his teeth were bared and he was growling and barking. Mrs Rabbit had her eyes closed and was pleading,

"Please, Mr Dog, please let me go." Jackdaw wasted no time; down he swooped. He flew around the dog's head, flapping his wings in its face, shouting at the top of his voice, "CAW, CAW, CAW." He dug his claws into the dog's head. "Run Mrs Rabbit," Jackdaw cried, "run now, I'll keep him off you." Mrs Rabbit needed to hear no more. She ran as fast as her legs could carry her. She didn't stop until she got to her home. She ran in and slammed the door behind her panting hard. Mr Rabbit rushed over to her.

"Whatever's the matter?" Mrs Rabbit sat down. When she'd caught her breath she told Mr Rabbit what happened. When she finished he asked, "Did you see what happened to Jackdaw?"

"No," she said, "I didn't look back, I just kept running."

"I must go and find him," said Mr Rabbit.

"Please be careful," said Mrs Rabbit. Mr Rabbit nodded and left the house. He stopped at Sammy and Jackdaw's tree. He called to Sammy. Sammy looked out.

"Hi Mr Rabbit, is something wrong?" Mr Rabbit explained as quickly as he could about Mrs Rabbit, the dog and what Jackdaw did to help her.

"Do you think you could run up to Jackdaw's nest to see if he is there? I'd like to know he's safe and to thank him."

"Of course," said Sammy and off he raced up to Jackdaw's branch.

"Jackdaw," he called, "Jackdaw old pal, are you there?" But there was no sound. Sammy looked inside the nest and saw it was empty. He ran back down the tree. "There's no sign of him," he told a worried Mr Rabbit.

"I must look for him," said Mr Rabbit, "he may need help."

"You're right," said Sammy. "I'll come too; I can look from the trees."

On their way, they met Brock Badger and Freddy Fox. When Mr Rabbit told them what had happened, they joined in the search. Sammy enlisted the help of the group of birds Jackdaw had seen earlier.

Everyone searched until the moon was high in the night sky. Eventually Mr Rabbit called everyone to him. "It's no use, we will have to wait until morning now. Let's go home and rest. We'll meet at Sammy Squirrel's tomorrow morning. Agreed?" Everyone agreed. They were all very tired, so off they went to their homes feeling very guilty about how they had treated Jackdaw that day. As Sammy climbed into his hole, he turned and told Mr Rabbit,

"if we find him safe and sound I will never moan about his singing again."

"Neither will I," said Mr Rabbit and they both went home to bed.

Early next morning, everyone met under Sammy and Jackdaw's tree. Sammy climbed down to the ground where the animals and birds were talking about the best way to find Jackdaw when suddenly there came a voice from the tree. "Is there something wrong? If it's been noisy it wasn't me, I'm never going to sing again." It was Jackdaw. Everyone looked at him, then Sammy said,

"Jackdaw, where have you been? We were searching for you last night but it got too dark. That's why we're all here, we were going to continue to look for you, but you're here and we're so happy to see you back. What happened?" Everyone listened intently as Jackdaw told them about the previous day's events, about how everyone told him how horrible his voice was and how he decided to leave the wood, then when he saw Mrs Rabbit and the dog,

"When Mrs Rabbit ran, I kept attacking the dog until he ran away," continued Jackdaw, "but I was so worn out it was all I could do to fly to Farmer Giles' barn. I came back this morning to collect my twigs to build a nest in a new tree. Thank you all for looking for me but as you can see I'm quite all right. I'll be on my way now, goodbye." But as Jackdaw turned to go, Sammy Squirrel stopped him.

"And where do you think you're going?"

"I'm leaving," said Jackdaw sadly, "so you don't have listen to me sing in the mornings."

"We don't want you to leave," said Sammy and all the other animals and birds chorused their agreement.

"Really?" said Jackdaw, "you really want me to stay?"

"Yes," they all said.

"And you can sing as loud and as often as you like," said Sammy.

"Oh thank you all my friends," said Jackdaw with tears in his eyes. He opened his beak and 'sang', "CAW, CAW, CAW." Everyone covered their ears.

"What have we let ourselves in for?" said Sammy and everyone laughed.

CHAPTER 2

MRS RABBIT'S NEW HAT

It was Mrs Rabbit's birthday. Mr Rabbit and all the little rabbits had a surprise present for her. Mr Rabbit had made her breakfast in bed and the children had given her their birthday cards. While she was drinking her carrot juice and reading her cards, Mr Rabbit and the children brought in a large box wrapped in shiny, silver paper with a big, red bow. "Happy Birthday," they all chorused. Mrs Rabbit clasped her paws together with delight. She shook the box and looked at her children with a big, beaming smile.

"What is it?"

"Open it, open it," all the children said. Mrs Rabbit began unwrapping the present carefully. She didn't want to tear the paper it was so pretty. "Hurry, hurry," cried the children.

"All right, all right, I'm getting there," said Mrs Rabbit, laughing. When she took the lid off the box, she could not conceal her pleasure. "Oh!" she exclaimed, "look at This," taking a pretty hat out of the box; she had tears in her eyes. "It is beautiful, and just the hat I wanted, how did you know?" The children laughed. Mr Rabbit smiled.

He had seen his wife look at the hat a few times in Mrs Prickle Hedgehog's Hat Shop and had asked Mrs Prickle secretly to put it aside for Mrs Rabbit's birthday. There was also to be a party on the Saturday, but Mrs Rabbit had known about that.

After all the excitement had died down, Mrs Rabbit got dressed and put on her new hat. "It looks lovely on you," said Mr Rabbit.

"Can we go for a walk, Dad," said Rufus Rabbit.

"Oh yes, let's," said Jenny Rabbit, "so Mum can show off her new hat."

"Why not?" said Mr Rabbit. He offered his arm to Mrs Rabbit. "Shall we go?" he said. She smiled and nodded, she put her paw through his arm and off the family went. It was a lovely day and Mrs Rabbit held her head high so all the forest animals and birds could see the hat at its best. Mrs Stoat and Mrs Weasel were one of the first to see it.

"What a lovely hat Mrs Rabbit," said Mrs Weasel.

"Thank you," said Mrs Rabbit, "my husband and children bought it for my birthday."

"Well, happy birthday," said Mrs Stoat.

"Thank you," replied Mrs Rabbit, "we're just off for a

walk, see you later." Mr Rabbit nodded and the children waved goodbye.

When the Rabbit family were out of earshot, Mrs Weasel turned to Mrs Stoat. "Of course, it doesn't suit her, not with that colour fur anyway, more my sort of colouring, don't you think?" Mrs Stoat decided not to answer but smiled at Mrs Weasel. She felt sorry for her. Mrs Weasel's husband was a nasty animal and was quite horrible to his wife most of the time. She knew Mrs Weasel was jealous of Mrs Rabbit, but she still remained friends with her. Everyone needed a friend, that was Mrs Stoat's motto.

Meanwhile, Mr and Mrs Rabbit and the children were enjoying their walk in the forest. Mrs Rabbit's hat was the centre of attention. Brock Badger and Freddy Fox had said how pretty it was. Mrs Rabbit beamed with pride. Sammy and Jackdaw came down from their tree to see it and wish Mrs Rabbit a happy birthday. "I love getting presents," said Jackdaw, "especially birthday presents, but I think I love birthday cake even more." He gave Mrs Rabbit a sheepish grin. "I don't suppose you have any birthday cake?" Mr and Mrs Rabbit laughed.

"Not at the moment," said Mrs Rabbit, "but there is a party on Saturday, so there will be plenty of birthday cake for you then."

"Great," said Sammy, "we will definitely be there, won't we Jackdaw?"

"Oh yes," replied Jackdaw, rubbing his belly and already thinking about birthday cake.

"See you Saturday. We have a few more animals to invite," said Mrs Rabbit, and the Rabbit family went on their way. The family were passing the cornfield on their way to the duck pond when Mrs Rabbit said, "Wait a moment, I want to invite Freda Fieldmouse. I'll see if she is in." She hopped over to Freda's house and called, "Yoohoo Freda, are you there?" A small head appeared at the door.

"Hello Mrs Rabbit, this is an unexpected pleasure, how are you?"

"I'm very well thank you. I've come to invite you to my birthday party on Saturday, I hope you can make it?"

Freda smiled, "Of course I can make it. That is a lovely hat, a present from the family?"

"Yes," said Mrs Rabbit proudly, "see you on Saturday."

"Certainly and thank you for inviting me" said Freda.

"Not at all, I'm off to see Dora Duck now, goodbye." The family were waiting patiently for her to return.

"Did you see Freda?" asked Mr Rabbit.

"Yes, and she will be coming on Saturday," replied Mrs Rabbit. "I hope Dora Duck can make it too." They walked towards the duck pond. On the way, Mr Rabbit turned to Mrs Rabbit and asked,

"Why didn't you ask Mrs Stoat and Mrs Weasel to your party?" Mrs Rabbit looked at him.

"I will ask Sarah Stoat, but I didn't want to ask in front of Winnie Weasel."

"Winnie seems nice enough. It's her husband who's the rogue," said Mr Rabbit. Mrs Rabbit laughed.

"Don't you believe it, I bet she couldn't wait until our backs were turned to talk about us, you are right about her husband though." They reached the duck pond.

"There's Mrs Duck," said Billy and pointed to the middle of the pond where Dora Duck and her four ducklings were diving for food. Mrs Rabbit called out to her.

"Hi Dora," and she waved. Dora Duck looked towards the bank. When she saw Mrs Rabbit she called the ducklings to her and the family swam towards the bank.

"I'm sorry to disturb your lunch," apologised Mrs Rabbit when Dora and her family waddled ashore.

"No problem," Dora assured her, "the children like to see their friends during the holidays; back to school soon."

"Not soon enough," laughed Mrs Rabbit. They started to chat while the children played together. Mr Rabbit lit his pipe and went to find Dora's husband, Dan Drake.

"Hello Dan," said Mr Rabbit.

"Hello Ron, lovely day."

"Yes it is," replied Mr Rabbit.

"What brings you out here?" said Dan.

"The wife's birthday today, having a party on Saturday, just wanted to see if you and the family can make it."

"I don't see why not," said Dan Drake, looking over at Dora Duck who was walking over to them with Mrs Rabbit.

"Are we off then?" said Mr Rabbit. Mrs Rabbit smiled.

"The children are getting hungry. Dora, Dan we'll see you all on Saturday."

"Of course," said Dora. She spoke to Mr Rabbit. "That is a beautiful hat you and the children have bought Rosy." Mr Rabbit smiled.

"Thank you, see you on Saturday." Rosy and Ron Rabbit called their children to them and off they set homewards. They turned around to wave goodbye when suddenly a gust of wind came from nowhere and WHOOSH, it lifted Mrs Rabbit's new hat clean off her head.

"Oh no!" she cried, "My hat," and she reached up to try and catch it, but it slipped from her grasp. Mr Rabbit and Rufus chased it down the lane but the wind whisked it high into the air.

"I'll see if I can get it," called Dan Drake and he flew into the air, but every time he seemed to get close to the hat, the wind whipped it away. Then suddenly, as if by magic, the hat dropped to the ground and disappeared. "It must be somewhere near you," shouted Dan. Mr Rabbit and Rufus looked around but found nothing.

"We can't see it down here," Mr Rabbit shouted back.

"I'll fly around up here a little longer to see if I can find it."

"Thanks Dan," and Mr Rabbit waved him goodbye. Mr Rabbit and Rufus returned to a very upset Mrs Rabbit.

"Did you find it?" she asked.

"Not yet Rosy, but Dan is going to keep looking while I take you home," said Ron Rabbit.

"No, no, it's all right. You help Dan look for my hat and I'll take the children home to get something to eat," replied Rosy Rabbit.

"You sure you'll be all right?" asked Ron Rabbit, concerned.

"I'll be fine" said Rosy, "now go and help look for my hat," and she shooed him away.

Ron Rabbit made his way to the duck pond where he met up with Dan Drake. "Any luck Dan?" he said.

"Sorry Ron, I don't understand it, there's no sign of it anywhere." Ron Rabbit thought for a while.

"You don't think it's stuck in a tree somewhere?"

"No," said Dan, "I could see all the treetops from up there and it wasn't in any of them." It was a puzzlement to the two animals, but there was someone who wasn't puzzled at all. Listening in the bushes was Wally Weasel and he found the two animals' conversation highly amusing. The reason he found it so funny was because he had Rosy Rabbit's hat. Earlier he had been rummaging around in the undergrowth and had heard the commotion. Peaking through the bushes, he had seen the Rabbit family and Dan Drake trying to catch the hat. He timed his moment perfectly. Just as the wind pushed the hat down towards the ground, Wally Weasel struck out his hand and whipped the hat into the bushes. He then dove into the undergrowth and waited. As Ron Rabbit and Dan Drake tried to decide what to do next, Wally Weasel made his way back home.

When he reached his house, he pushed the door open and called to his wife, "You 'ere?" he snapped. Winnie Weasel came out of the kitchen.

"Where else would I be?" she said solemnly. Wally Weasel threw the hat at her.

"Don't say I never give you nuffin'," he coughed and wiped his nose on the back of his paw. Winnie looked at the hat.

"Where did you get this?" she asked.

"I just got it, all right?" he growled at her, "what's the problem?"

"It's just that I saw Rosy Rabbit this morning with a hat just like this," she said.

"AND?" he challenged and looked at her through narrow eyes.

"And nothing." Her voice went quiet. "I was just saying."

"Well don't. If you don't want it I'll have it back," and he stretched out his paw.

"No, no, it's fine, thank you," said Winnie Weasel. Wally Weasel smiled a sly smile.

"Now go and get my dinner," he snapped and Winnie slunk off into the kitchen.

Meanwhile at the Rabbits' home, Ron Rabbit was explaining to Rosy Rabbit that try as they might, the hat was well and truly lost. Rosy Rabbit shrugged her shoulders and with tears in her eyes said, "Never mind, you did your best, I just wish it hadn't been my birthday present."

"I know," said Ron Rabbit and gave her a cuddle.

The next day, news of Rosy Rabbit's lost hat was known all over the forest. "It's such a shame" said Dora Duck to Freda Fieldmouse, "she must be so upset, it was her birthday present you know." Freda nodded. Sarah

Stoat was passing by the two friends on her way to Winnie Weasel's house. Dora Duck called her over. "Did you hear...?" And she began to explain what happened. When Dora had finished, Sarah Stoat shook her head.

"That is so sad; I'll keep my eyes open for it," and went on her way.

When she reached Winnie Weasel's house, she knocked on the door. When Winnie opened the door, Sarah looked at her in amazement. Winnie smiled. "Like my hat? My Wally got it for me." Sarah continued to stare at Winnie.

"That's Rosy Rabbit's hat!" explained Sarah.

"It is not, it may look similar but it's not hers," snapped Winnie.

"Oh come on Winnie, you know it's Rosy's. Where did Wally get it from?" Sarah was trying to get Winnie to admit the hat wasn't hers.

"I have no idea what you are talking about," snorted Winnie. "Wally gave this to me last night, it's obvious me and Rosy have the same sort of hat."

"You can't believe that," said Sarah. "Rosy lost her hat yesterday afternoon. Don't you think it's strange your

Wally turns up with a hat that looks like her hat on the same evening?"

"No I don't," snarled Winnie. "This is my hat not Rosy's, okay?"

"I'm sorry Winnie, but until you accept that is Rosy's hat, I won't be coming round anymore," and away Sarah Stoat went with Winnie Weasel's scathing words following her.

"Who cares? I don't need your friendship, I don't need anyone."

Over the next few hours, Sarah explained to most of the animals what she had tried to get Winnie to do. "You must tell Rosy," said Brock Badger "she has a right to know." Sarah sighed.

"Yes, you're right. I'll go and see her now."

Sitting in Rosy Rabbit's house, Sarah Stoat told her what had happened. "I'm sorry," she ended, "I'm afraid she just wouldn't listen to me."

"Thank you for trying Sarah," said Rosy, "but there's not much any of us can do, if she insists the hat is hers. I mean, her husband could have bought one the same for her."

"Considering your hat was a one off, that's highly unlikely and no one will believe that," stated Sarah. "Sorry again Rosy, I better go now."

"Before you go," said Rosy, "I'm having a party on Saturday. Can you come?"

"Of course, I will," said Sarah and off she went, feeling slightly guilty about Winnie but at the same time, she felt better for telling Rosy.

Winnie Weasel, however, was not having a very good day at all, which is what she should have expected as she had lied about the hat. She just couldn't see why the animals were turning their backs on her, it was her hat after all... As she walked by Brock Badger and Freddy Fox they tutted very loudly and turned away from her. The same thing happened every time she met one of the forest animals. Even Sarah Stoat who she thought was her friend had been mean to her. "I don't care," said Winnie defiantly and walked passed the group of animals with her head held high in the air. It wasn't until she got home, that she let herself relax. Taking off the hat, Winnie put it on the table and stared at it. She knew the hat was Rosy Rabbit's, she knew it the minute Wally Weasel had given it to her, but there was nothing she could do about it now, was there? No one was talking to her and the damage was done.

The next day, Winnie didn't venture out of her house. She couldn't, she felt guilty and sad. She couldn't face going into the forest knowing all the animals didn't want anything to do with her. Her absence was noticed, but no one was worried about her. Nobody, that was, except Sarah Stoat. She knew Winnie had done a bad thing and she was still angry with her, but she couldn't help feeling sorry for her. 'I'll just pop round to see if she's all right,' she decided and off she went.

When Sarah Stoat came to the Weasels' house, all was quiet. She knocked on the door. There was no answer. She knocked again; there had to be somebody home. A curtain moved and a voice came from behind the window. "What do you want?"

"I've come to see if you're all right," said Sarah.

"Well now you know, you can go." Sarah turned to go, when she heard a muffled sob from inside the house. She went to the back door.

"Winnie," she called, "Winnie, let me … maybe I can help."

"Why would you want to help me?"

"I thought," said Sarah slowly, "that we were friends." There was a silence that seemed to go on for ages, then the door clicked open. Sarah Stoat walked in. Winnie Weasel threw herself into Sarah's arms.

"Oh Sarah," she sobbed, "what am I going to do? No one's talking to me, everybody hates me and all because I was too stupid and jealous to give back the hat. I did want one like it so much." Tears poured down her face. Sarah Stoat sat her down and made her a cup of tea. When Winnie had calmed down, they began to talk.

"Are you sorry for what you've done?" asked Sarah.

"Oh yes," said Winnie. Sarah looked at her. "Honestly," said Winnie, "I just wish I knew what to do."

"You must give the hat back," said Sarah.

"And how do I do that without looking a fool?" sulked Winnie.

"You swallow your pride; you can come with me tomorrow." Winnie Weasel looked at Sarah.

"You mean go to Mrs Rabbit?"

"Yes," said Sarah.

"We'll go together okay?"

"All right," said Winnie and she managed a smile.

"I'll call for you," said Sarah, as she left the house and Winnie nodded and waved her goodbye.

The next day was very busy for Rosy Rabbit. She was getting everything ready for the party. She was so busy running here and there she almost forgot about Winnie Weasel and her hat, but as the time got nearer for her friends to arrive, Rosy wished that she had her hat; it would have gone so well with her new dress. Rosy gave herself a shake. No point in moping; this was her birthday party and she must be cheerful. She looked out of the window and saw the first of her friends arriving. 'Better get out there and be the hostess,' she said to herself and off she went into the garden.

Further down the lane, Winnie Weasel and Sarah Stoat were walking slowly towards the Rabbits' house. Winnie was worried. "What shall I say?"

"That will be up to you, but apologising would be a good start," said Sarah.

"Yes, yes, you're right," agreed Winnie and she straightened her dress. As they got near the Rabbits' house, Sarah could see that most of the animals had arrived. Winnie noticed too and stopped. "Why is everyone here? Are you trying to humiliate me?" She turned to go. Sarah grabbed her arm.

"They're here for Rosy's birthday party. I thought it was about time everyone found out that you're a nice animal really," and she gently pulled Winnie towards the house. As they got to the gate, everyone stopped talking and looked at the pair standing there. Rosy Rabbit walked over to them.

"I'm sorry Sarah but I don't remember inviting your friend here."

"If you'll just give her a minute Rosy, please?" Sarah looked pleadingly at Rosy. Rosy nodded her head.

"All right," she said. Sarah tapped Winnie on the arm.

"I'll just be over here," and she walked away leaving the two animals together. Winnie glanced around her. Sarah gave her an encouraging smile.

"I know I'm not welcome here," began Winnie, "but I honestly didn't want to upset anybody, it's just that you've got it all, a lovely home, a husband and children that love you. Sometimes I think my Wally can't stand the sight of me. Anyway, that's neither here nor there. When he came home that night and gave me the hat, it's the first time he's ever given me anything. I tried to kid myself he'd actually bought it but I knew deep down it was yours but I was too proud and too jealous to give it back to you." She paused, "Until now that is. I know nothing I've said excuses the way I've behaved but I am so sorry and you all have every right to hate me." It was the longest speech Winnie had ever made. As she passed a box to Rosy Rabbit the animals began to whisper amongst themselves. Rosy opened the lid and looked inside and there was her hat. When she looked up, Winnie Weasel was not there.

"Where did she go?" asked Rosy. Sarah Stoat pointed down the lane. There was the lonely figure of Winnie Weasel, shoulders slumped, head bowed, walking slowly down the lane. "WINNIE WEASEL," shouted Rosy, "just you hang on a minute." Winnie stopped but didn't turn Around. Rosy Rabbit caught up with her. Winnie looked at her through tearful eyes.

"What's wrong now? The hat should be okay, I didn't damage it."

"The hat's fine," said Rosy. "Where are you going?"

"I'm going home," Winnie replied sadly.

"Why don't you come and join the party?" said Rosy Rabbit softly.

"But I ... I thought you all hated me." Winnie's voice was a whisper.

"Don't be silly. I admit what you did made me very angry but I didn't hate you, you silly animal, you did the right thing in the end. I can't talk for the others but I, for one, forgive you, so let's start again and try to be friends, agreed?"

"Agreed," said Winnie and walked with Rosy back to the party. She wondered how the other animals would react but she need not have worried. They all agreed that Winnie had done the right thing in the end and they were all prepared to give her another chance. They smiled and began chatting to her. Sarah Stoat stood beside her friend, feeling very pleased that Winnie would no longer be without the friendship of the other animals. Winnie Weasel took Sarah to one side.

"You were right," she said quietly. "In this case, honesty was definitely the best policy." Then off she went to talk to the animals. Sarah Stoat shook her head, laughed to herself and wondered if Winnie really had learnt her lesson.

CHAPTER 3

FREDDY FOX'S NEAR MISS

The sun was setting on the horizon and Freddy Fox was just leaving Brock Badger's house where he had been having tea. "Isn't it a beautiful evening?" sighed Freddy.

"Yes it is," agreed Brock, "and so peaceful."

"Oh yes," said Freddy, "on that I do agree with you Brock my friend."

"It's at times like this I wish I could hold the picture in my mind and keep it forever," said Brock. Freddy laughed gently.

"That's very poetic."

"Mmm," mumbled Brock and they both laughed out loud.

"Well, Brock old friend, I'm off home now. This evening has been most enjoyable, I will see you tomorrow of course."

"If you can make it after lunch," replied Brock. "I have to visit my grandmother. I'd ask you along but she's not fond of foxes."

"I quite understand. After lunch it is then, see you," and Freddy went on his way.

"Bye," Brock called after him.

Next morning, Brock rose early. His grandmother was quite a grumpy animal and was particular about him being on time. She lived on the other side of the forest so it was a bit of a walk and Brock didn't like rushing, so as he had made sour, he had plenty of time to get to his grandmother's. He took a slow leisurely stroll through the forest. It was a brisk, fresh morning, the sun rays were just beginning to show through the trees and the streams of light made the dew on the grass glisten. The birds were singing, and the only other sound was the babbling of the brook. Brock Badger smiled. It was hard not to in all this serenity. 'Who could be moody on a morning like this?' he thought, and it seemed nobody was, because all the animals he met on his way greeted him with bright smiles and a cheery, 'Good morning'.

Brock got to his grandmother's house with plenty of time to spare. Her house was hidden behind a thicket bush near the end of the brook; a large field was on the other side. Brock knocked on the door and called, "It's me Gran, Brock." A gravelly voice answered from inside,

"Push the door, it's open." Brock went inside.

"Hello Gran," he said.

"Well, come and sit down then." She glanced over at the clock. "Nice and early too."

"I try to be on time," said Brock. "How are you Gran?"

"I'm fine, apart from my old bones play me up something wicked at times. You're looking well. It's a bad old state though when I have to invite my own grandson to come and see me. I suppose you've been hanging about with that foxy friend of yours," and on she went. Brock sighed. 'Here she goes again,' he thought. "Strange that, you being friends with a fox, would never had happened in my day, not natural, not natural at all. If your father was here he'd put a stop to it."

"Yes Gran," interrupted Brock irritably. "Freddy is not a bad sort."

"Freddy is it?" her voice rose a little. "Well, let' s hear no more about this Freddy or whatever he's called. Do you want some tea?"

"Yes please." Brock followed his gran into the kitchen. "Have you seen much of Mrs Mole?" he asked.

"Yes actually, she came around yesterday," his gran replied. She put the tea on the table and a plate of cakes. "She was saying she has to be extra careful at the moment."

"Why's that?" Brock asked.

"Well," said his gran, "apparently the farmer has hired a mole catcher."

"My goodness," said Brock and nearly spilt his tea.

"Yes, two of her cousins have already been caught."

"That's terrible." Brock was shocked.

"As I said to her," continued his gran, "if you go around making hills in their nice green lawns it's bound to make them angry."

"But they can't help it, it's what moles do," replied Brock.

"Anyway, I told her she'd be better off staying in the forest. No one would mind then."

"You're probably right," agreed Brock. "Do you think Mrs Mole will come and stay in the forest?"

"I think she will, she knows there not much choice." Brock took a chocolate cake. He was just about to take a bite when the house began to shake; there was a low, rumbling sound which seemed to be coming nearer. 'It can't be thunder, surely?' thought Brock. The sound got louder and louder until Brock knew what it was. Horses. But they never usually entered the forest. The animals sat in silence while the house shook all around them until the sound began to fade and then disappeared. Brock looked at his gran who shook her head. "Humans," she said.

"But that was horses," said Brock.

"And who do you think was on the horses, you silly boy?"

"But why come through the ..." Brock didn't finish. The sound of hooves could be heard again but there was also a new sound. Brock knew this sound and he shivered in fright. It was dogs: hunting dogs. He glanced across to his gran but she seemed not to notice. 'Humans and hunting dogs meant one thing: an animal was going to lose its; life, but what animal?' thought Brock. It obviously wasn't the badgers or they would be running for their lives. "Who are they hunting?" Brock looked at his gran. She coughed uncomfortably.

"Well, they're using dogs and they wear red coats. They've been over yonder for a day or so now. Maybe they couldn't find what they wanted there." Brock was horrified. Humans in red coats and dogs meant one thing: fox hunters and now they were in the forest. Then the awful reality hit him: FREDDY.

"I'm sorry, I have to go Gran." He headed for the door.

"What now? I've hardly seen ..." Brock didn't let her finish.

"Yes now. I'm sorry, I don't mean to be rude but I've got to warn Freddy."

"You'll probably be too late," said his gran unfeelingly.

"I do hope not," he said and he ran out of the door.

Little did Brock know that he didn't have to worry about Freddy. Earlier, Freddy had been merrily cleaning his house when there was a knock at the door. There stood a pigeon. This pigeon worked for Pigeon Post and he delivered the mail. "Fly-o-gram." he said.

"Okay," said Freddy, taking the letter from the pigeon.

"I'll wait for a reply," he said. Freddy went inside and opened the letter, it read, 'COME QUICK- MUM ILL- NEED HELP LOVE FROO'. Freddy quickly wrote a reply and gave it to the bird.

"Deliver it now please," he said.

"Will do," replied the pigeon and off he flew. Freddy went back inside. 'I must leave a note for Brock.' He stuck it to his front door, the note said, 'BROCK, HAVE GONE TO SEE MY MUM, WILL EXPLAIN TOMORROW - FREDDY'. After making sure his door was locked, he went on his way. His mother lived in the valley quite near the village and it took a couple of hours to get there, even for a fast fox like Freddy. Freddy had been gone for about thirty-five minutes when unbeknown to him, racing through the forest like vultures swooping on scraps of food were the huntsmen and their dogs. All the animals in the forest scattered in terror, the birds stopped singing and the only sound was that of the galloping horses, the huntsman's horn and the fearful baying of the hounds. But Freddy was unaware of all of this. He was too busy rushing to see his mother. He had now arrived at the lake that separated Farmer Giles' land from the valley. There was no way of going around so he had to go across. Luckily Freddy was a good swimmer.

About the same time that Freddy was swimming the lake, the dogs had found Freddy's house and were jumping about excitedly. The head huntsman shouted to the others. "It must be here, the dogs have found the scent." Then he ordered the dogs, "SEEK." The dogs were frantic. They tore down Freddy's door and destroyed his house in their desperate efforts to find him. "He's not here," said the head huntsman, "he must have heard the dogs; he can't be far." Suddenly one of the dogs let out a howl and off he ran, the other dogs raced after him. "They've got the scent," cried the man and away they galloped.

Meanwhile, Brock was moving as fast as he could. "I must get there," he panted. He was aware of the quietness of the forest. His steps became slower as he neared what used to be Freddy's house. He stopped beside the pile of wood and briar. "Freddy, Freddy," he called. No answer. Brock's heart sank. He knew calling was useless. He began to sift through the rubble. The note Freddy had left for Brock was nowhere to be seen, so poor old Brock had no idea his friend was safe. He didn't know that the hunters and their dogs were at the lake, the dogs were sniffing here and there. "They can't pick up the scent anymore; we've lost him." The head man waved the others away. "Might as well call it a day and go home. He won't be back now he knows we've been here." The horses galloped away, followed closely by the dogs, but all this was totally unknown to Brock who was very upset over his missing friend.

He went back to his house, head bowed, feeling utterly miserable. Rosy Rabbit had crept out of her burrow to make sure it was safe for the children to go out and play, as had most of the other animals, when Brock passed. She noticed how sad he looked. "Brock, what's the matter?" He didn't seem to hear her, he just wandered on towards his house mumbling. Rosy hopped beside him. "Brock, what is it?" Brock looked at her sadly and shook his head.

"Poor Freddy" and off he shuffled. Rosy was confused.

"What about Freddy?" she asked, but all Brock kept repeating was,

"Poor Freddy." He went into his house and shut the door nearly in Rosy Rabbit's face. She shrugged her shoulders and went back to her house none the wiser about what Brock was talking about. She had seen Freddy leave his house before the dogs had come and couldn't understand why Brock was so sad, but Brock wouldn't talk to her so there wasn't much she could do.

Meanwhile, Freddy had reached his mother's house and had discovered that his sister Froo had overreacted. His mother had a bad cold and was surprised but pleased to see him. "What are you doing here?" she asked. Freddy frowned at Froo.

"My sister over there sent a fly-o-gram saying you were ill and that you needed help so here I am." His mother gave Froo a stern look.

"Tish and Twaddle," she said. Freddy smiled. His mother always said that when something was rubbish and silly. "I've only got a cold." Froo looked sulkily at Freddy.

"What about this morning then?" She looked across at her mother.

"What about this morning?" asked Freddy.

"Mother was coughing and spluttering. She couldn't catch her breath. You nearly passed out." Froo stared at her mother who was laughing

"You silly girl, I had taken a sip of tea which went down the wrong way that's all." Freddy began to laugh as well.

"Oh very funny, I'm sure," said Froo and she stomped out of the room.

"Well now I'm here, I might as well stay and go home tomorrow, if that's okay?" said Freddy.

"That would be lovely," his mum replied. The next morning Freddy rose early.

"If I go after breakfast I'll be in time for lunch with Brock."

"You must bring him with you when you come again," said his mother.

"Yes, I will," he replied. He ate his breakfast, said goodbye to his mother and sister, then headed home.

When he reached the edge of the forest, he looked up to see where the sun was. "Mmm," he said, "11.30. I'll be in time for one of Brock's delicious lunches," and on he went. Walking through the forest, Freddy could feel that there was something different. There were a lot of broken branches and trampled flowers, the ground was turned over and there were a lot of animal tracks around, only Freddy couldn't tell what they were as they seemed to be all on top of one another. Still the forest was calm enough he thought and headed for his house.

What faced him as he got to where his home should have been shook him to the end of his brush. He stood there open mouthed. It took him a few minutes to speak. "What on earth happened to my lovely home?" He pushed aside the bits of wood. "Who has done this? I'll go to Brock, he'll know." Off Freddy went to Brock's house.

Inside his home, Brock was sitting in his rocking chair feeling very, very, sad, when there came a knock at the door. He didn't feel like answering it. "GO AWAY," he shouted.

"Brock! Brock old friend, it's me open the door." Brock stared at the closed door. No! It wasn't possible; he was hearing things. Was he hearing Freddy's voice in his grief? "What's the matter Brock, why aren't you opening the door? It's me, Freddy." Brock jumped out of his chair Could it be true? He ran to the door and threw it open. There was Freddy in all his foxy glory. Before Freddy could open his mouth, Brock flung his arms around his friend and hugged him tight, talking so fast that Freddy had to stop him mid speech. "Whoa, Brock old friend, please let me breathe – what is all this?" Brock stepped back.

"Freddy, Freddy, where have you been? Come in for tea and tell me all. I have been so sad; I thought the dogs had got you." Freddy stared at him.

"Dogs! What dogs? And what happened to my house? I go to my mother's for one day and everything goes to pot."

"So that's where you were, thank the Great Spirit of the Forest." Brock was overjoyed.

"Didn't you see my note?" asked Freddy.

"It must have got lost in the rubble when the hunt destroyed your house."

"Hunt! What hunt?" Brock laughed.

"Sit down old friend and we'll talk over lunch; you can stay with me until we rebuild your house."

"Thank you so much Brock," said Freddy. "I am so lucky to have a friend like you."

"Not at all," replied Brock, "I'm the lucky one. You never know how much friendship means to you until you think you've lost it." The old friends smiled at each other and sat down to have a long chat, content in the knowledge that there would be many more to come.

CHAPTER 4

BILLY'S FIRST DAY AT SCHOOL

It was Billy Rabbit's first day at school. He wasn't too sure about it; he knew Jenny, Rufus and Lisa went and they seemed to have fun, but he'd never been away from home before. He went everywhere with Mummy and baby rabbit, but now it was time to cut the apron strings and go out into the big wide world ... well, Billy always did have a vivid imagination. Rosy Rabbit brushed his fur and straightened his tie. She stepped back and smiled at him. "You ready to go then?" she said softly. Billy hung his head, his eyes welled with tears.

"No," he said firmly. Lisa laughed at him.

"Come on Billy, you'll like it." Jenny put her arm around him. "Look Billy," she said, "we all feel scared of things we're not sure about, but Lisa is right, you'll make lots of new friends and don't forget, we'll be there." Billy shrugged her arm away.

"I'm not scared," he sulked.

"Anyway," said Rosie Rabbit, "I'll be taking you so you don't have to worry." Rufus picked up his school bag.

"I heard Dora Duck's youngest was starting today as well," he said. Billy looked at him.

"I didn't know Danny was going too." Rufus laughed.

"Feel better now?"

"A bit," said Billy. Rosy gave him a hug.

"Have you all got your lunches?"

"Yes Mum," they said together.

"Right, let's be off then."

Jenny, Rufus and Lisa left first, Rosie Rabbit put the baby in his pushchair and held out her paw for Billy. For a moment he stood there not wanting to take it, because he knew when he did there would be no turning back. Rosy smiled at him, kissed his cheek, took his paw and gave it a gentle tug. "Come on," she said, "you don't want to be late on your first day." Walking down the path, Billy said brightly,

"If I'm late can I come home?" His sisters and brother Laughed.

"I'm afraid not," replied his mother. His face dropped and he kicked a stone with his foot.

"I won't like it," he mumbled. Rosy Rabbit sighed. She was beginning to wish the morning was over. The other children had started school with no problems and she had thought Billy would be the same, but she was obviously wrong.

The school came in sight, the sound of children shouting and playing happily echoed all around. Lisa, Jenny and Rufus ran ahead calling to their friends. Billy's steps got slower and slower until Rosy Rabbit was almost dragging him. "Billy - please, you're making my arm ache; it won't be so bad, honestly."

"Good morning Rosy." Dora Duck's voice made her turn her head.

"Hello Dora," she replied, "How's your Danny been?"

"To be honest Rosy, he's been a bit tearful. He's putting on a brave face now though." Dora smiled at her son who sort of smiled back. "What about Billy?" she asked. Rosy Rabbit ruffled Billy's head. He was now standing close behind her, clasping her dress.

"He's a bit scared, he was hoping we'd be late and thought he would come back home." Dora laughed.

"They do get some funny ideas don't they?" Billy looked up at his mum and stood away from her.

"I told you I wasn't scared," he said, not very convincingly. Suddenly, another rabbit came up to him. It was a little girl.

"Hello," she said, "what's your name?"

"Billy," he said quietly.

"Hello Billy," she said, "my name is Bonny, Bonny Bunny. Are you starting school today?" Billy looked at the little bunny who was annoyingly cheerful. "Oh goody," she said excitedly, "so am I, maybe we can sit together, wouldn't that be nice?" Billy just looked glumly at her. "There's my Mummy, see you in class," and off she bounced. Billy didn't reply. Rosy Rabbit frowned at him.

"She was very nice, wasn't she?"

"No," said Billy.

"You weren't very kind to her, were you?"

"So, don't care," he said stubbornly.

"Oh Billy, what am I going to do with you?" Rosy said.

"Take me home," he mumbled. Rosy looked at Dora and shook her head.

"Kids" she said. Dora laughed.

"Don't I know it? Danny go and talk to Billy." She leant over and whispered in Rosy's ear. "Maybe the two of them can help each other." Rosy Rabbit nodded, feeling hopeful. The two animals looked on as the boys stood side by side staring at the ground. Danny Duck was the first to talk.

"Are you scared? – I am a bit."

"No – well, maybe, just a bit," admitted Billy. Just at that moment, Tawny Owl rang the school bell. Billy and Danny jumped at the sound and both looked pleadingly at their mothers.

"Off you go," said Rosy Rabbit gently and she gave Billy a kiss on the cheek. His arms came up and he clung to her neck. She took his arms off her neck. "Come now," she said firmly, "get into line with the others," and she pointed to the line of children, waiting to go in. Billy walked slowly away from her looking back every now and then. Danny Duck followed behind with his head bowed. Billy could hear him sniffing. He looked back at his mother and looked away quickly. Rosy raised her paw and waved. She choked back the tears she could feel rising in her eyes and turned to go. Dora Duck touched her arm.

"I'll walk with you, fancy a cup of tea?" Rosy nodded.

"That would be nice." She looked at Dora and noticed two tears rolling down the duck's beak. "It's still hard isn't it?"

"What's that?" Dora asked.

"Letting go," replied Rosy. Dora smiled.

"Yes, it is," and both animals wiped tears from their faces.

Meanwhile, at school Billy and Danny were standing in line with the other young animals. Billy was relieved to see he wasn't the only one who was feeling horrible. He turned to Danny. "Are you okay?"

"I'm not too bad now," he said, "I wonder what happens next?" No sooner had Danny finished speaking, Tawny Owl said,

"Now, we shall go to our classroom. When we go in you will see desks and chairs, on the desks there are labels, on those labels are your names, see if you can find the desk with your name on it. Don't worry if you can't find it at first, come and ask me if you really don't know where to sit. Now, are we ready? let's go inside in a nice orderly line." All the children entered the school silently. Most were too amazed to speak as they had never seen the inside of the building, but once inside the classroom, they found their voices again, eagerly chatting and running around the desks looking for their names. Billy, who was determined not to like being at school, stood by the door and refused to move. Tawny Owl watched him but said nothing. Suddenly Danny rushed up to him and grabbed his arm. "Quick, I've found our desks, we're next to each other." Billy pulled his arm away but Danny didn't mind, he ran to where his and Billy's desks were. "Look! This one's mine and that's yours." Billy moved slowly towards his desk. Inside his tummy he felt a flutter of excitement, but he ignored it.

"I won't like school," he muttered to himself. When he reached his seat he sat down and stared at the desk. Suddenly, a voice called him from across the room.

"Billy, Billy, yoo-hoo." Billy reluctantly looked up recognising the voice. It was Bonny, she was grinning broadly and waving wildly.

"Bonny, please sit down," Tawny Owl's voice echoed across the room, the many voices in the room quietened to whispers. "Now," she continued, "on your desks you will notice a large box. In this box are paper and crayons, when you are all sitting down you will take a sheet of paper and a crayon. Who," said Tawny Owl, walking slowly around the room, "knows the alphabet?" Quite a lot of hands went up in the air. Billy very nearly put his up but snatched it down quickly. "Not just a little bit but all from A-Z." Tawny Owl looked straight at Billy. Billy closed his eyes tight and began to silently pray,

'Please Great Spirit of the Forest don't let her ask me', but the Great Spirit must have been busy because as he opened his eyes, Tawny Owl's smiling face was level with his. "Billy, do you know the alphabet?" Billy shuffled his feet and shook his head. Tawny Owl tried again. "Do you know some of it?" Billy looked to the floor and shook his head again.

"No," he said in a quiet voice. Tawny Owl smiled sweetly at him and said softly,

"Come on, stand up and give it a go." Billy slowly pushed his chair back and stood up. He held onto the desk, his legs were shaking, he looked around the classroom, everyone was looking at him, he felt like he needed the toilet. He took a deep breath. 'Right, let's go,' he said to himself and began to say it.

"A-B-C-D-E," he closed his eyes and carried on, "F-G-H-I-J ..." until he got to 'Z'. He opened his eyes. Tawny Owl was clapping her wings and all the children joined in.

"Well done Billy," she said. "Here, this is for you" and she handed him a lollipop, "and this gold star goes on your card for excellent work." She held the card in the air for the class to see. "You all have these cards and every time you do good work you will get a gold star." Billy was annoyed with himself. He was actually feeling pleased with himself but kept his face sullen. He noticed he no longer needed the toilet. He sat back down; Danny slapped him on the back.

"That was brill, how did you know all that?"

Billy smiled. "Rufus taught me." There was no doubt about it, Billy was beginning to like school. The children took paper and crayons and Tawny Owl went through the alphabet with them, getting them to draw pictures that went with the letters. Everyone had fun doing this, even Billy. A bell rung and Tawny Owl said,

"It's playtime, off you go." They all ran to playground. Billy and Danny spoke to some of the other boys and they decided to play football. They were halfway through the game when Bonny's voice reached Billy's ears.

"Hi Billy." He looked over. She was standing with some of the other girls; he carried on without answering her. Bonny called to him again. "Billy, Billy." Billy stopped playing and said to the boys,

"Hang on a minute." He walked over to Bonny. She really was a nuisance. "What do you want?" he asked gruffly.

"I just wanted to say that you were excellent in class," she said, "in fact, we all think you were great, don't we girls?" The others nodded their heads in agreement. Billy sniffed.

"Was that it?" Bonny looked bewildered.

"I don't know why you're being so nasty Billy Rabbit; I'm only trying to be friendly."

"Then be friendly to someone else," snapped Billy, but wished he hadn't said it when he saw tears well up in Bonny's eyes.

"All right then I will." She spun round and stomped off with the rest of the girls. Billy felt bad. He called after her.

"Bonny, please I'm ... sorry," but his words fell on deaf ears. He hung his head and sighed.

"Billy, come on, are you playing or not?" The boys were calling him. He returned to the game and forgot about Bonny until the bell rung and they went back to the classroom.

Across the room, Billy saw Bonny. She looked over at him and he smiled at her. She turned her nose up at him and looked away. Billy was sorry for what he had done but it looked like he was going to have a hard time convincing Bonny. The rest of the afternoon went well.

Billy no longer felt the need to pretend he didn't like school because he did. The lessons were fun, Tawny Owl was nice, he had made new friends and lost one he thought sadly. But he was determined to make Bonny his friend again; he just had to find the right time. To Billy's relief, the right time came sooner than he expected. Tawny Owl called for the children's attention. "For this part of the lesson," she said, "I need you to pick a partner to work with." Billy's paw shot up in the air. Tawny Owl looked at him mildly surprised. "Yes Billy, what is it?"

"Please Miss, I would like Bonny as my partner." Bonny started to protest.

"I don't want to." Tawny Owl silenced her with a wave of her wing.

"Quiet please Bonny. Billy, you've given me an idea. I'd like the rest of you boys and girls to partner up together, boy girl boy girl, you understand?" The rest of the children nodded but they were not too keen. Danny Duck whispered to Billy,

"That's your fault; working with girls, yuk!"

"Shh," said Billy, "I'll tell you why later, okay?" Danny shrugged his shoulders.

"Okay." He looked around the room and noticed a little girl stoat. She glanced at him shyly. Danny went over to her. "Want to be my partner?"

"Oh, yes please," she said quietly. He sat down and they began to talk. It turned out that she was called Sally and her mother was Sarah Stoat. Meanwhile, Bonny had sat next to Billy but she was refusing to talk to him. When all the children were paired together, Tawny Owl drew a picture of a bridge on the blackboard.

"Now," she said, "who can tell me what bridges are built from?" Many hands went up in the air, including Billy's. Tawny Owl pointed to a little hedgehog in the front. "Yes Henry?"

"Stone Miss."

"Well done," said Tawny Owl, "and what else?" She looked around. "Sally." Sally stood up.

"Metal Miss."

"Very well done, yes, bridges can be built from stone and metal like iron and steel, you can also have wooden bridges. Now, in front of you there are blocks, cardboard, plasticine and some plastic cups. What I would like you to do is build a bridge. When you have done that, we shall see whose bridge can hold the most weight, okay? Now you can start." Billy turned to Bonny who was sitting with her arms folded.

"What shall we start with?" Bonny turned away from him.

"Please Bonny," Billy pleaded, "I am so sorry. I didn't mean to be horrible; can we please be friends? I promise not to be horrible again, honest." Bonny turned around slowly and looked at him.

"All right Billy Rabbit, I forgive you." Billy put out his paw.

"Friends?" Bonny smiled and put her paw on top of his.

"Friends; now let's build this bridge." The children thoroughly enjoyed building their bridges with the items they were given. Some of the bridges collapsed as soon as anything was put onto them, but they all managed to build bridges that could hold something. Tawny Owl went to each pair of children in turn and asked them questions about their bridge. When she got to the last pair the bell rang.

"That's the Home Bell children. Have you enjoyed your first day?" The children agreed it had been fun. "Because you have all done excellent work, you shall all be given a star. Collect your coats and you can all have a lollipop from my jar. Nice orderly line now and I'll see you tomorrow."

Outside in the playground, all the mothers were waiting. Billy ran over to his mum. She gave him a big hug. "How was your day?" she asked anxiously.

"Great," replied Billy, "be back in a minute, Mum" and off he ran, much to the surprise of his mum.

"Where is he off to?" asked Dora Duck.

"He's talking to Bonny," said Danny. Rosy Rabbit raised her eyebrows, amused at Billy's change of heart. Billy came running back waving his paw and shouting,

"Bye Bonny, see you tomorrow." Bonny waved back and skipped away with her mum. Rosy Rabbit and Dora Duck began to walk home, Billy and Danny followed behind chatting excitedly about the day's events. Billy told Danny why he had chosen Bonny to be his partner.

"I'm glad you're friends again," said Danny. "I made friends with Sally Stoat too."

"It's fun making new friends isn't it?" said Billy.

"Yes," replied Danny, "even if some of them are girls." Both boys laughed and ran ahead of their mothers. At the crossways everyone said goodbye. Billy and Danny arranged to meet there the next morning so they could walk together with their brothers and sisters. They agreed school wasn't as bad as they thought it would be.

At home, Lisa, Jenny and Rufus were doing their homework. Billy sat down to read a comic. Rufus looked at him and said, "Not scared any more, little brother?" Billy pulled a face at him.

"I wasn't scared in the first place; school was no problem." His brother and sisters looked at each other and laughed. Billy stamped his foot. "Stop laughing." Rosy, who had heard the conversation came over to Billy and gave him a hug.

"Billy Rabbit," she said, "you are a big fake and as stubborn as your father." Billy smiled at her.

"I know," he said, "but I wasn't scared of school ..." Rufus began to say something but stopped when Billy finished with, "... in the end," and everyone laughed.

CHAPTER 5

THE CONKER GAME

The leaves on the trees were abundant with autumn colours: all shades of brown, red and orange. The sun was still warm but the breeze had a hint of coolness about it. This was a sign that winter was slowly creeping up on the forest. Sammy Squirrel was busy collecting acorns, Jackdaw was filling up his nest with feathers and bits of sheep wool to make it warmer. The Rabbit family were also making sure their food cupboard was full. Freddy Fox and Brock Badger had decided to spend the winter months together. Winter could be a lonely time, and if heavy snow came, it was difficult to leave your house. They had decided to stay at Brock's house as it was covered by thicket and was on a slight hill, so there was no chance of flooding when the thaw came. The Duck family had flown to a warmer country, the other animals had waved them off, a little envious of where they were going. Mrs Prickle Hedgehog had closed her hat shop, Mr Stoat had shut his DIY shop, Tommy Toad sold his last book of the day and returned to his pond; the only shops left open were Harry Hare's Fruit and Veg and Mrs Partridge's Bits and Pieces. The animals had agreed that Harry should open his shop, especially after what had happened to Rosy Rabbit with Farmer Giles' dog. Harry was the best at collecting fruit and veg and the fastest when it came to running from trouble. Mrs Partridge did not mind staying open through autumn. Winter did not bother her; as it got colder, her feathers began to change colour until she was as white as the snow itself.

Whilst all the animals prepared themselves for the coming winter, Ferndale Forest itself began to undergo a change. The leaves on the trees slowly fell from the branches covering the ground below like a soft blanket, the evergreens became greener and bushier, the sharp prickly balls of the horse chestnut fell to the floor where Billy, Rufus, Lisa, Jenny, Bonny and Henry scooped them up. They opened them carefully and inside was a shiny, brown nut called a conker. "Wow," exclaimed Billy, holding up a large conker nearly the size of his paw, "look at this. Bet no one finds one as big as this." Jenny smiled at him.

"I'm sure there will be many like that." Billy laughed and picked up a conker from her pile; it was very small compared with his.

"Well, this isn't one."

"You're right Billy," replied Jenny, "that isn't one, but if we look hard enough I'm sure we'll find one like yours." Billy secretly hoped they wouldn't as he wanted to be the one with the biggest conker. Before they could look for more, Rufus ran up to them.

"Let's play a game of conkers, we have got loads." Excitedly the animals agreed.

"I'll run home and get some string," said Lisa and she started off to the house.

"Bring a screwdriver as well," Jenny shouted after her.

"Okay," replied Lisa and off she ran. Not long after, Lisa could be seen skipping down the lane with a bag in her paw. Rufus took the bag from her and looked inside. There was a screwdriver and string that had been cut into equal lengths. "Daddy cut them for us and he told me to tell you to be careful with the screwdriver." Rufus began to put holes in his conkers. He then did the others. When he thought he had finished with Billy's pile he noticed the large one that Billy was still holding on to.

"Give it here Billy and I'll put a hole in it for you."

"No," snapped Billy and held the conker to his chest, "I don't want to." Rufus put his paws in the air.

"Okay, there's no need be like that." Jenny came over.

"It really doesn't matter if Billy doesn't want to use that conker, he has plenty of others." Everyone agreed.

They all began to sort their conkers into sizes and tied the string to them. It was decided that as Rufus and Jenny were the eldest, they would play each other first, Bonny and Lisa were next and then Henry and Billy. They were to knock the conkers together until one broke then they would swap partners. In the first game Rufus beat Jenny, Bonny beat Lisa and Billy, to his delight, beat Henry. They changed partners and carried on playing. The young animals were enjoying themselves so much they didn't realise the time until Mr Rabbit came looking for them. "Come on you lot, it's time for your tea, and your mothers are looking for you two," he said to Bonny and Henry. They followed him up the lane; they all agreed to meet the next day and carry on with the game. Bonny and Henry's mum were waiting for them outside the Rabbits' house.

"See you tomorrow," they called to each other.

Inside the house, Rufus was boasting about his victory over Jenny and Bonny. He lovingly rubbed his conker.

"This is the best conker ever." Jenny stuck her tongue out at him.

"The game isn't over yet," she said. Rufus laughed.

"I beat Henry and Lisa," said Billy proudly to his father. Rosy Rabbit put their tea on the table.

"Just remember, it's only a game," she reminded them. Their father nodded.

"Your mother's right, but more importantly when you compete in any game, whether it is serious or for fun, you lose or win with goodwill." Rosy put her paw on his shoulder.

"Well said dear." The young rabbits nodded their heads in understanding. Billy ate his tea in silence. After he had finished he turned to his father.

"I understand what you meant Daddy, but is it all right to feel pleased when I win?" Ron Rabbit smiled at his son.

"Of course it is, you can be proud of yourself when you win, but always win fairly." Billy nodded.

"I will Daddy."

After their tea, the children helped their mother clear up, then they went to their room. They sat on their beds and talked about the conker game. "How will we arrange the game tomorrow?" asked Jenny. "Will it be the same as today?" Rufus thought for a bit.

"We may have to change the way we've been playing to make things fair for everyone." Lisa and Billy yawned; they were feeling very tired. Their mother entered the room.

"Time for bed, wash your faces and don't forget to brush your teeth, I'll be back to check on you all in ten minutes, okay?"

"Okay Mum," they said.

After washing and brushing their teeth, Billy and Lisa could hardly keep their eyes open. Jenny and Rufus helped them put on their pyjamas, Lisa fell asleep as soon as her head touched her pillow, Billy stayed awake just long enough to take his conker from the dressing table, tucking it under his pillow. He fell asleep and dreamed of being a winner in a conker competition and being given a big gold cup. Rufus and Jenny spoke in whispers. "My idea," he said, "is, if we play with one partner until only one has a last conker, then the ones left play each other and the last one left with the only conker is the winner, what do you think?"

"I think it's a very good idea, Rufus," replied Jenny, "but will the others agree?"

"Well it seems the fairest way, unless someone else can think of something better."

"Let's find out tomorrow," said Jenny. Just at that moment their mother came in, she checked on Lisa and Billy.

"Come on you two," she said quietly, "time for some sleep, goodnight."

"Goodnight Mum." Jenny and Rufus snuggled down in their beds, closed their eyes and hoped the morning would come quickly.

Next morning, the children were up early. "You're all eager," stated their father.

"Need to get out," said Rufus between mouthfuls of breakfast.

"Oh and what exciting things have you got planned?" asked their mother.

"We need to finish our conker game," replied Billy. "I dreamt my conker was the best and I won a gold cup." Billy's eyes were shining. His father smiled at him.

"Nice dream then?" Billy nodded. Jenny and Rufus grinned at him. Lisa sighed,

"I wish I had dreams like that, I never win anything."

"You never know, my love, this may be your chance." Her mother gently touched her face.

"I doubt it," sulked Lisa, "I never won anything at the school sports day and I got beaten twice yesterday." Billy looked at Lisa and gave her a hug.

"It's okay, it's only a game," he said. Lisa hugged him back and smiled.

"I know, shall we go now?"

The Rabbit children left the house to meet their friends. Henry and Bonny were already at the end of the lane waiting impatiently, when they saw them. They waved wildly,. "Hurry up, we've been waiting for ages."

"I could hardly sleep," said Henry, "I just wanted to come out and play again."

"I hope you don't mind," began Rufus, "but Jenny and I thought the game would be fairer if we play it like this," and he began to explain what he and Jenny had been talking about before they went to sleep. When he finished, he looked at them and said, "What do you think?" Henry spoke first.

"Sounds okay to me."

"And me," said Bonny. They waited for Billy and Lisa's answer. Billy crossed his arms.

"Why do you always make the rules?" he said grumpily.

"I don't," replied Rufus.

"Yes you do," moaned Billy, "and anyway, who said it was your game anyway?"

"I never said it was my game, we just thought that way would make things fairer on everyone." Rufus shrugged his shoulders and raised his arms. He didn't understand why Billy was so annoyed. Jenny once again came to the rescue.

"Well Billy, if you can come up with a better idea we'll play it your way okay; it's only a game remember?" Everyone was silent for a while. Bonny let out a loud sigh.

"I'm bored. If we're not going to play then I'm going home, this is really silly." Henry agreed with her.

"I'm going too. I didn't think playing a game was going to cause this much bother." Lisa turned to Billy.

"This is your fault acting like a spoilt child - Bonny and Henry want to go home now."

"I'm sorry," he sulked.

"Have you got a better idea than Rufus?" Lisa snapped. She waited for an answer. "No, I didn't think so."

"All right Lisa, that's enough," said Jenny.

"Well," replied Lisa, "he gets on my nerves," and she turned her back on him.

"We've already wasted nearly an hour with all this silly bickering, now are we playing this game or not, Lisa?" Lisa nodded her head. Jenny turned to Billy. "Billy?" Billy looked around; everyone was waiting for him to answer.

"Yes, all right then." Jenny let out a sigh of relief.

"Thank goodness for that."

"Great," said Rufus "let's get on with it."

Rufus was playing Henry; Jenny was playing Lisa and Billy was playing Bonny. The children carried on playing well into lunchtime. Rosy Rabbit took some food down for them all. As she neared the clearing she could hear their voices, there was a mixture of groans and cheers. Rosy called to them. "Children, I've brought you something to eat." The little animals stopped what they were doing and ran to her. "How is the game going?" she enquired.

"I beat Jenny," said Lisa.

"I got beaten" sighed Bonny, "but it was a good game."

"Henry and Rufus still have to play." Jenny pointed to their conkers. "Neither of them seem to want to break."

"Sounds exciting," said Rosy Rabbit, "I will send your father to come and get you for tea later, okay?" Rufus, Jenny, Lisa and Billy nodded.

"Bye Mum."

"Bye Mrs Rabbit," said Bonny and Henry. After they had eaten, Rufus and Henry carried on with their game. The others looked on, cheering for both of them as they didn't want to take sides. Ten minutes had past. Rufus's conker began to crack. Henry swung his for another hit but missed. Rufus held his conker in the air and swung it down towards Henry's one. It struck it hard, there was another cracking sound, they both looked at their conkers.

"Mine's all right," said Henry. Rufus noticed another crack in his but it hadn't broke. He swung his conker at Henry's again and missed.

"Oooo," said the others. Henry raised his conker and aimed it at Rufus's. There was a groan from Rufus as

Henry's conker hit the other one. Rufus's conker split in two and fell to the ground. The girls and Billy clapped and cheered.

"That was an excellent game," said Jenny. "Well done Henry." Rufus and Henry shook paws.

"Who's left?" asked Billy. Jenny thought for a moment.

"You, Lisa and Henry. How are we going to do this?" The little animals sat and thought for a while. "I've got an idea," said Jenny. They all looked at her. "You all draw sticks."

"What?" they all said.

"Listen," Jenny had their attention. "I'll collect three sticks. Two will be the same length and one will be smaller, whoever ends up with the same length sticks play together and the other one plays the winner of that match." The animals agreed it was a very good and fair idea. Jenny found some sticks and held them in her paw covering the bottoms so that they all looked the same size. Henry went first. He pulled out a long stick. Lisa went next and did the same, so Billy was left with the small stick.

"So I play the winner of you two?" he smiled. Henry and Lisa's match began; back and forth it went with both animals' conkers holding up strong. Then Lisa's conker hit Henry's hard and it broke. Lisa jumped up and down with excitement. Henry smiled.

"That was a really good game, well done Lisa." That left Billy to play Lisa. The brother and sister stood in front of each other, the conkers hanging on their string. Lisa went first; her conker hit Billy's hard but neither conker gave way, four more times she hit Billy's conker but it still didn't crack. On her next turn she missed, so it was Billy's go. He was just as lucky - three times he hit Lisa's conker but missed on his fourth try. Backwards and forwards continued the game with both conkers not breaking; then suddenly Lisa's conker developed a small split which got bigger every time Billy hit it and it seemed like Billy was never going to miss. Billy went to hit Lisa's conker once more. He swung down and his conker narrowly brushed Lisa's making it move slightly. He raised his conker for another hit. Lisa pulled her one away.

"You missed, it's my go now."

"No it isn't," protested Billy, "your conker moved." Both animals looked at their elder brother.

"I don't know," he said. "Whatever decision I come up with will make one of you unhappy, so I don't want to say."

"But as the eldest you have to," said Jenny. Rufus looked uncomfortable.

"Okay, as Lisa's conker did move a little, Billy you take another shot." Lisa was amazed.

"What?" she gasped.

"Billy will have another go," replied Rufus. Lisa's face was like stone. She held out her conker, she glared at Billy as he took his shot, Billy's paw was shaking a little as he swung his conker down, it missed. Lisa looked at Billy in disbelief. Billy looked like he couldn't believe he had missed either, his conker spun around in the air. When it stopped spinning, Lisa raised her conker in the air. Down it swung, it hit Billy's with a resounding CRACK; pieces of conker flew everywhere but whose was it that broke? Everyone looked at the little animals. Lisa and Billy held up their strings. Both conkers had broken to pieces but as if it were clinging to life, Lisa's string still had half a conker hanging from it. Rufus held her paw in the air. "I declare Lisa the winner." Lisa couldn't believe it, she squealed with delight and jumped up and down. Everyone cheered - even Billy.

"That was brilliant Lisa," he said.

"Thank you Billy," replied Lisa and she gave him a big hug.

The children walked home and talked about the conker game. When they got to the Rabbits' house, Rufus said, "What do we do next?" Henry shivered as the wind blew through the forest.

"It'll be winter soon," he said, "I feel snow in the air."

"I love snow," said Bonny.

"I have an idea," Jenny smiled, "why don't we build snowmen?"

"Brilliant idea Jen," said Lisa.

"I bet I build the biggest one," Billy said smugly. The animals looked at him, picked up a handful of leaves and threw them all over him, laughing. Billy laughed, brushing leaves off his fur. "I was only joking; can no one take a joke?"

"I'm sure you were, Billy" replied Henry, smiling. "I'm off home. Come on Bonny I'll walk you to your house. Thanks for a great day everyone," and off the two animals went to their houses.

The Rabbit children went inside and told their mother and father about their day. Lisa proudly let them know how she won, and she held out what was left of her conker. Billy went into the bedroom and pulled his big conker from his pocket. He jumped as Lisa came up behind him. "You should have used that," she said softly.

"Why?" asked Billy.

"Because it's a champion size, you would have won easily with that," she replied.

"Oh I don't know so much," he said, "it doesn't matter now. You won fair and square, as Daddy says, that's how you play the game isn't it?" Lisa nodded. Billy could be quite bright at times she decided, she kissed his cheek. "What was that for?" he asked surprised.

"Just for you being you," and she turned to leave the room.

"Wait a minute, Lisa," he called. Lisa turned back.

"What is it?"

"Here, this is for you," and he handed her his conker.

"Why ..." she started to ask.

"A champion conker for a champion sister." He felt silly saying soppy things, even if he meant them. Lisa held the conker tight.

"Oh Billy," she said, "you are sweet … sometimes," and they both laughed. "Come on," said Lisa, putting her arm through his. "Let's see what's for tea," and they both left the room, friends together and as close as brother and sister should be … until next time.

Acknowledgements

The publishers and authors would like to thank Russell Spencer, Matt Vidler, Susan Woodard, Janelle Hope Leonard West, Lianne Bailey-Woodward, Laura Jayne Humphrey and Katie Major for their work, without which this book would not have been possible.

About the Publisher

L.R. Price Publications is dedicated to publishing books by unknown authors.

We use a mixture of both traditional and modern publishing options, to bring our authors' words to the wider world.

We print, publish, distribute and market books in a variety of formats including paper and hardback, electronic books, digital audiobooks and online.

If you are an author interested in getting your book published, or a book retailer interested in selling our books, please contact us.

www.lrpricepublications.com

L.R. Price Publications Ltd,

27 Old Gloucester Street,

London, WC1N 3AX.

020 3051 9572

publishing@lrprice.com